# A Tr____
# of Tricks

## Patrick Skene Catling

*Illustrated by*
*MARK FOREMAN*

*For Diana*

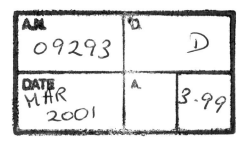

First published in Great Britain 1994
by William Heinemann Ltd
an imprint of Reed Consumer Books Ltd
Michelin House
81 Fulham Road
London SW3 6RB

AUCKLAND · MELBOURNE · SINGAPORE · TORONTO

Printed in Great Britain by William Clowes Ltd

A school pack of BANANA BOOKS 67-72 is
available from Heinemann Educational Books
ISBN 0 435 00098 5

# Chapter 1

IT WAS THAT exciting time of the year when people begin wondering about Christmas presents. Diana Blake thought of all sorts of wonderful things she would like to have, but nothing as surprising as the present her mother and father planned to get for her. In a magazine, there had been a small advertisement:

> African orphanage seeks good
> home for Malaika. She
> is a healthy, well-behaved four-
> year-old of sweet character,
> high intelligence and great
> charm. Her name means Angel.

'Malaika,' said Mrs Blake to her husband. 'What a lovely name! Don't you think she would be a perfect little sister for Diana?' Mr Blake wasn't so sure, but in the end he agreed to adopt Malaika and pay for her flight from Africa to England. Diana was allowed to stay away from school on the day Malaika was due to arrive.

The Blake family got to Heathrow Airport, near London, in plenty of time to meet the plane.

'I hope she'll like me,' Diana said.

'I'm sure you two will get along just fine,' Mrs Blake assured her. 'Of course, she may be rather shy at first, the dear little thing. But we'll soon make her feel at home.' The Blakes waited for a long time, looking carefully at all the people passing by, but they didn't see any very little girls. Mr Blake asked an airline official about Malaika. The man checked some papers and went away to make a telephone call.

He came back smiling.

'She has definitely arrived,' he said, 'but you will have to go to the freight department. She will need to have a health inspection before you can take her.'

Puzzled, Mr and Mrs Blake and Diana hurried to Freight. There they found two men in overalls unfastening the side of a large wooden packing case. It had a small opening, a sort of window, with bars.

'I don't understand ...' murmured Mrs Blake.

'We've got Malaika here,' one of the men said. 'Are you the people who've come to collect her?'

The other man reached into the open crate and grabbed the end of a rope.

He gave it a tug ... and out came Malaika.

The Blakes were amazed.

Malaika was a baby elephant!

'She's in great shape,' said the Health Inspector. 'Here you are, just sign here and you can take her away.'

Diana thought Malaika was by far the best present she had ever had. She chattered about her all the way home, sometimes turning to look and see if the big van carrying the precious baby elephant was still there. Mr and Mrs Blake were too stunned at first to say much.

'Perhaps we could keep her in the garage,' Mrs Blake suggested.

'We'll have to,' Mr Blake said. 'She may be as well-behaved as they say, but she certainly can't live in the house. It's lucky we've got a double garage and a small car.'

# Chapter 2

MALAIKA'S BODY WAS like a small well-rounded sofa. Slightly taller than Diana, she had strong, thick legs, big, floppy ears she could flap, and a muscular, sensitive trunk. Her trunk was like a nose as long as a hose-pipe that could reach the ground or bend to grip and lift things. Her wrinkled hide was grey with a touch of pale brown. Another elephant would have called her beautiful.

Mr Blake seemed a bit anxious at first, because Malaika was the first elephant he had ever had to order about. But he soon found she was gentle and obedient and readily allowed him to guide her into her half of the garage.

'Isn't she sweet?' Diana said. 'The way she's looking up at you, Daddy! Her dark, shiny eyes; her long, curly eye-lashes!'

'Yes,' Mrs Blake agreed. 'She's pretty all right. But I wonder what we're supposed to give her to eat?'

'I know what to do,' said Mr Blake. 'I'll telephone the zoo for advice.'

A keeper who took care of elephants told him that they are strict vegetarians. They never eat meat.

'Elephants know what is good for them,' the keeper said. 'Not only are they the world's biggest land animals, they are also the cleverest. They are very sensible, but not fussy. They have hearty appetites. Give your elephant hay and oats and vegetables and fruit. At her age, about forty kilos a day should be enough. And, of course, plenty of water, both inside and out. Elephants like regular baths and a good scrubbing.

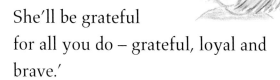

She'll be grateful for all you do – grateful, loyal and brave.'

Mr Blake hung up the telephone and sighed.

'Forty kilos a day!' he exclaimed. 'That's about ninety pounds, almost six and a half stone! That's more than Diana weighs! It sounds as if Malaika is going to be expensive to feed. Where are we going to get all the fodder she's supposed to have?'

Mrs Blake thought of looking for the right sort of food supplier in the Yellow Pages telephone book. They found one under 'Animal Foodstuffs' who said he would deliver the food every day. 'I'm afraid Malaika is going to require a lot of looking after,' Mr Blake said.

'I'll look after her!' Diana promised. 'I'll get up extra early and wash and feed her before I go to school. Then, as soon as school is over, I'll come straight home and play with her every afternoon. And at weekends I'll ...'

'Yes,' Mr Blake interrupted, 'that sounds all very well. We'll see how things work out.'

# Chapter 3

DIANA KEPT HER word. Every morning, she cleaned out the garage, gave Malaika a thorough scrubbing, put down fresh straw, untied a bale of hay, and filled buckets with oats and water. Every afternoon, she did it all again, with great pleasure, and gave Malaika bananas and apples to eat.

When Malaika had finished her afternoon meal, Diana took her out for exercise, even if it was raining. When it rained, Diana wore her yellow raincoat, rain-hat and wellies. Malaika enjoyed rain.

Men, women and children stopped and stared in amazement as Diana walked past, calmly leading Malaika along the streets to the park.

'Hey, miss!' a park-keeper said the first time. 'Have you got permission to bring that into the park?'

'Her name is Malaika,' Diana said. 'Who has to give us permission?'

'The park-keeper took off his cap and scratched his head, thinking hard. He took out a book and looked through the

park rules and regulations. He frowned for a few moments, then smiled.

'Well,' he said, 'I don't know. There's nothing here against bringing elephants into the park, so it must be all right.'

In the park, children ran from all directions to look at Malaika close up.

She wrapped her trunk around Diana's waist. Although Malaika was only four years old, she was already very strong. She easily lifted Diana and carefully placed her on her own back to give her a ride.

Naturally, the other children asked for rides too. Malaika willingly gave them all a turn.

Diana made many new friends.

'I wish I had an elephant,' one boy said to her. 'You are so lucky.'

'Yes,' she said. 'I know.'

At home, Diana told her mother about the excitement of elephant-riding in the park.

'Sitting up there, looking down at everyone, I felt like an Indian princess,' Diana said.

'I hope it's safe,' said Mrs Blake.

'Oh, yes, it's quite safe. Malaika isn't at all silly. She didn't go too fast, and she let me hold on to her ears.'

When Diana had finished her

homework, she always went to the garage to check that Malaika was comfortably settled for the night. Then she gave Malaika her supper – oats, fruit, lots of fresh water, and a lump of sugar. She loved sugar. Diana never gave her more than one lump though, because Mrs Blake said they did not want to spoil Malaika's teeth. Malaika had twenty-four teeth for grinding up her food, as well as two tusks, which were already several inches long.

As England is usually colder than Africa, Diana covered Malaika's back with a duvet when it was time for her to go to sleep.

Everything was peaceful. But then one evening something frightening happened.

# Chapter 4

A FEW DAYS after Malaika's arrival, the Blakes went to the Garden Centre and brought home a large Christmas tree. It was too big to take inside the house, but it fitted perfectly in the shelter of the front porch.

Diana enjoyed helping to decorate the tree. They had some silver tinsel, cotton-wool snow, ornaments from past years, and a string of coloured electric lights.

'This tree needs more lights,' Mr Blake decided. He brought two more long strings, and soon every part of the tree was decorated with red, blue, pink and yellow lights, with a white star on top.

Diana was impatient for the blue-grey dusk of evening, and the first switching-on of the tree-lights. She let Malaika out of the garage, so that she, too, could watch. Mrs Blake, Diana and Malaika stood on the path in front of the house and Mr Blake pressed the switch.

Diana and her mother exclaimed 'Ooh!' and 'Ah!' at the brilliant colours, but Malaika moved back a couple of steps.

'She's frightened,' Mrs Blake said to Diana. 'I don't suppose she has ever seen anything like this before. You'd better take her back to the garage.'

After supper, the Blake family left

the house to take Christmas presents to
some friends. Malaika, looking through
the garage windows, watched the
Blakes go, well wrapped up against the
howling wind. 'This is a strange, cold
country!' she thought.

She was comforted by the colourful glow of the Christmas tree lights. But, a few minutes after the car had gone, an extra-strong gust of wind blew the tree down. There was a crackle of blue sparks from the lights and the tree caught fire.

Fire frightens all animals, but Malaika was both brave and quick-thinking. She knew she had to do something right away or the flames

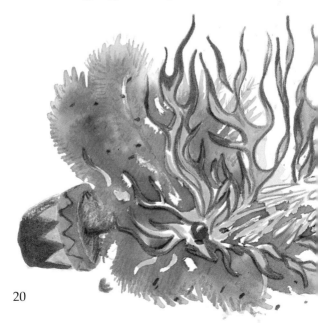

would leap higher and set the house on fire. So she forced open the garage door.

Within seconds, she got to the gold-fish-pond, sucked up water with her trunk (being careful not to suck up any fish), and strongly blew the water out again, spraying the fire. There was a great hiss of steam. It took three well-aimed trunkfuls of water to put out all the flames.

The Blakes' next-door neighbour, who spent a lot of time peeping out through her curtains, saw Malaika's prompt, heroic action. Soon after the Blakes returned and saw their ruined tree sagging in a pool of blackened water, their neighbour telephoned to tell them what had happened.

'If it hadn't been for that elephant,' she said, 'you would have lost a lot more than a Christmas tree. You would have lost your home; and, if the fire had spread, I might have lost mine too.'

The Blakes were very grateful.

'Isn't Malaika wonderful?' Diana said, selecting a delicious ripe banana from the kitchen fruit-bowl. She went to the garage and gave Malaika the banana and a big kiss on the cheek. 'Thank you, Malaika,' she said, 'for being such a clever elephant.'

Fortunately, when Mr Blake made another trip to the Garden Centre, they still had a few good trees left. He also bought a new set of tree decorations, but this time he secured the tree firmly and didn't use so many lights. Christmas was saved!

# Chapter 5

MALAIKA'S NEXT ADVENTURE happened in the middle of a dark, moonless night, shortly after Christmas. The Blakes were in their beds and Malaika was on her bed of straw in the garage. They were all asleep.

Malaika was awakened by a scraping sound in the lock of the garage door, a click, and then a creak as the door slowly opened. Torch-light revealed a man wearing a black balaclava and carrying a sack. He probably planned to steal the Blakes' car. When he entered the garage, the light of his torch dazzled Malaika as she climbed to her feet.

'An elephant!' the burglar exclaimed. Astonished and angry, he lifted his heavy metal torch up high and bashed it down on Malaika's forehead. The vicious attack would have knocked a human to the floor. But Malaika's head was so strong that the blow was no worse to her than the sting of a mosquito.

Once again in an emergency her trunk was useful. She trumpeted and

trumpeted as loudly as she could. An elephant's trumpeting at its loudest is a mixture of a roar and a shriek, much louder than the loudest burglar-alarm in the world and can be heard for miles.

Malaika woke the whole

neighbourhood and terrified the burglar. He turned to run, but Malaika moved too fast to let him escape. With her strong trunk, she seized him so tightly that he could not move his arms. No matter how hard he struggled, there was nothing he could do to break free from Malaika's powerful grip.

Mr Blake and Mrs Blake and finally Diana, wearing their dressing gowns and slippers, rushed out to the garage to see what was wrong. Mr Blake quickly ran back inside the house and telephoned the police.

A few minutes later, a police car, with its siren wailing and its blue light flashing, came speeding to the scene. Two police officers jumped from the car and ran to the Blakes' assistance.

'We've been trying to catch this man

for a long time,' one of the policemen said. In the burglar's sack there was some valuable silver stolen from a local house earlier that night. Again, Malaika was a heroine! But that was only the beginning of her fame. There were other, even more interesting things she could do with her trunk.

# Chapter 6

Elephants love music. One Saturday morning, when Diana had plenty of time to give the garage a specially thorough cleaning, she brought her portable radio with her. It was her pride and joy. Her father and mother had given it to her on her last birthday and she had used it every day since. There was a tape-deck that could make recordings.

Listening to one of her favourite pop groups while she swept the floor in time with the music, Diana noticed that

Malaika also was keeping time, by flapping her ears. The group got Malaika so excited that she suddenly joined in, playing her trunk like a trumpet. Malaika was really talented. She quickly picked up the tune, which was called 'Rocket Baby', trumpeted along with the other musicians, and finished with a long, loud, high note that made the windows rattle and Diana's hair stand up.

'Great, Malaika!' Diana shouted. 'I can't wait to tell my friends!'

When Diana brought some of her father's tapes to the garage, Malaika was eager to play along with them. Because an elephant never forgets, she soon knew a lot of fancy musical tricks.

'She's sensational!' said Peter Boysoe, one of Diana's school friends, who was a pop-music expert. 'You

31

ought to record her. I bet if you sent a Malaika tape to the BBC they'd play it on the radio.'

The BBC did even better than that. They sent somebody to interview Diana the following weekend. When they found that Malaika really was a talented baby elephant, the BBC broadcast a special one-hour TV programme to show her to the public.

Malaika was a tremendous success.

After a couple of broadcasts, she was given a pop group of her own—Malaika and The Ivories. There were two guitars, a keyboard, drums and Malaika on trunk. They played a new kind of music, which became known as African Rock. Their recordings and videos were played all over the world, night and day. They zoomed to the top of all the charts and stayed there. They sold millions of copies and Malaika won three important awards.

She became the most popular elephant that ever lived—and easily the richest. Fans wrote for her photograph. Soon there were Malaika dolls, Malaika T-shirts, Malaika chocolate bars, and even plastic Malaika masks, which people could wear if they wanted to look like her. This, by the way, is the first Malaika book.

Then one day a silver-grey Rolls
Royce arrived at the Blakes' house.
A large man wearing sunglasses and
smoking a long cigar offered Mrs Blake
$100,000 if she would allow Malaika to
be filmed for a TV soap commercial.

'What do you think, Diana?' Mrs
Blake asked.

'I'm not sure,' Diana said. 'Malaika's
already working hard. She's only four.
She may be getting a bit over-tired.'

'How about $200,000?' the man suggested.

'That's a lot of money,' Diana admitted. 'Maybe she wouldn't mind making just one commercial.'

The Malaika soap commercial is still talked about. It is one of the most famous commercials ever broadcast on television.

Malaika was filmed in a kitchen, where washing dishes with Brill Soap Powder was supposed to be such good fun that she trumpeted one of her most celebrated song-hits. Then she dipped her trunk into the soap-suds in the kitchen sink, raised her trunk again, and filled the air with soap-bubbles that were as big as balloons and glittered with all the colours of the rainbow.

But Diana knew Malaika well and understood that the little elephant was not really happy.

# Chapter 7

MALAIKA WAS NOW a millionaire. Mr Blake had saved her money in a bank account of her very own. But elephants are not interested in money. There was something else she wanted. The Blakes were always kind to Malaika and she loved them as much as they loved her. The trouble was that Malaika was growing up. She missed the great open spaces of Africa and the company of other elephants.

'Malaika isn't eating properly,' Diana told her mother one day. 'When I took her breakfast to the garage she was lying curled up in a corner, and her eyes were full of tears.'

'Oh, dear,' Mrs Blake said. 'I hope she isn't getting flu. I wonder whether I should call a vet.'

'I don't think she needs a doctor,' Diana said. 'I think she's homesick. She misses the hot sunshine and the grassy plains of Africa. And she misses bathing in the warm lakes with her friends.'

When Mr Blake returned from his office, the family sat around the kitchen table to talk.

'I'm afraid you're right,' he told Diana. 'You have had a lot of fun with Malaika, but the best thing you can do for her now is to let her go back to where she truly belongs.'

So Mr Blake went to arrange for Malaika's long journey home. He used some of Malaika's money to hire an airliner for a private flight, so the Blakes and Malaika could travel together in comfort from London to Nairobi, in the part of Africa where she was born.

Mr Blake gave the rest of Malaika's great fortune to the orphanage, so that they would have enough money to look after all the other baby elephants who had lost their parents. Elephants, like humans, cannot take care of themselves fully until they are grown up.

Diana did not feel sad about leaving Malaika, once she saw how happy she was to be back among other elephants in her own country. Diana kissed Malaika goodbye, and Malaika gave her

a sort of kiss back, with the soft tip of
her trunk.

'You have been a fine sister to
Malaika,' Dr McAuley, the director of
the orphanage, said to Diana. 'And you
have helped her and many more young
elephants.'

'We'll come to visit her during the summer holidays,' Mr Blake promised.

'Malaika will never forget you, Diana,' the director said. 'Never, never.'

Malaika trumpeted.